For Jane and Mischa and the rest of my family—
you make me feel gold
—L. R.

For S.C. for the endless encouragement,
and for J.M. for creating the space and time to make this book
—A. S.

BEACH LANE BOOKS • An imprint of Simon & Schuster Children's Publishing Division • 1230 Avenue of the Americas, New York, New York 10020 • Text copyright © 2018 by Lauren Rille • Illustrations copyright © 2018 by Aimée Sicuro • All rights reserved, including the right of reproduction in whole or in part in any form. • BEACH LANE BOOKS is a trademark of Simon & Schuster, Inc. • For information about special discounts for bulk purchases, please contact Simon & Schuster Special Sales at 1-866-506-1949 or business@simonandschuster.com. The Simon & Schuster Speakers Bureau can bring authors to your live event. For more information or to book an event, contact the Simon & Schuster Speakers Bureau at 1-866-248-3049 or visit our website at www.simonspeakers.com. • Book design by Sonia Chaghatzbanian The text for this book was hand-lettered by Aimée Sicuro. • The illustrations for this book were rendered in ink, watercolor, and gouache and assembled digitally. • Manufactured in China • 0518 SCP • First Edition • 10 9 8 7 6 5 4 3 2 1 • Library of Congress Cataloging-in-Publication Data • Names: Rille, Lauren, author. | Sicuro, Aimée, 1976 illustrator. • Title: I feel teal / Lauren Rille ; illustrated by Aimée Sicuro. • Description: First edition. | New York : Beach Lane Books, [2018] | Summary: Encourages the reader to enjoy all of the colors, representing feelings, that may be experienced in the course of a day. • Identifiers: LCCN 2017042954 | ISBN 9781481458467 (hardback) | ISBN 9781481458474 (e-book) • Subjects: | CYAC: Stories in rhyme. | Emotions—Fiction. | Color—Fiction. | BISAC: JUVENILE FICTION / Social Issues / Emotions & Feelings. | JUVENILE FICTION / Concepts / Colors. | JUVENILE FICTION / Stories in Verse. • Classification: LCC PZ8.3.R4714 Iaf 2018 | DDC [E]—dc23 LC record available at https://lccn.loc.gov/2017042954

I Feel Teal

Lauren Rille · Aimée Sicuro

Beach Lane Books New York London Toronto Sydney New Delhi

You're pink.

You're gray.

You're jade.

You're every golden,
warmy shade.

You're scarlet,

mauve,

and purpley too.

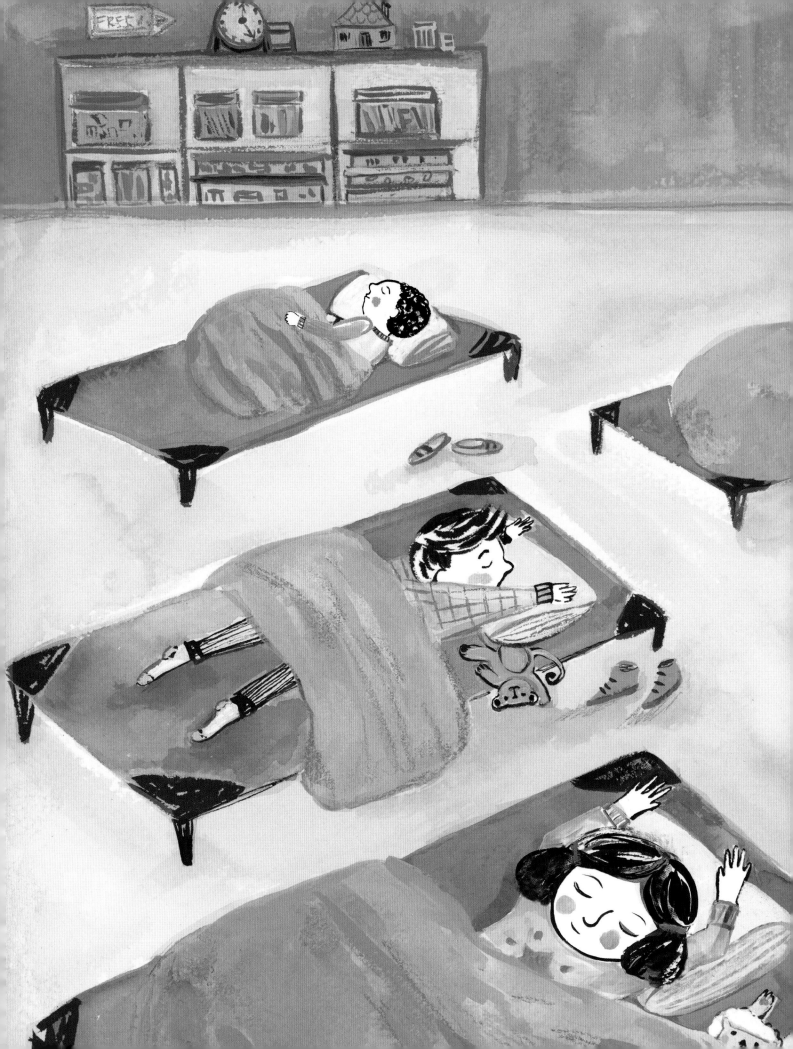

Lilac,

magenta,

a quiet ecru.

You're red

and orange.

Our Family Trees Pr

and blue.

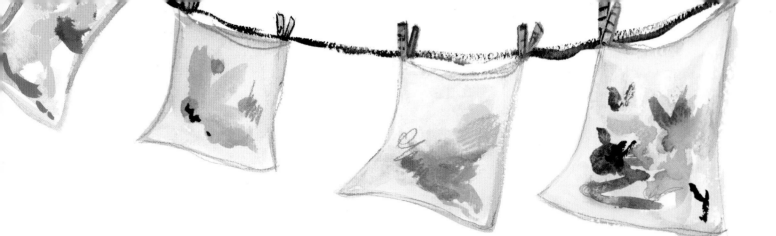

You're all the colors,

from hue to hue.

So when you feel them,
let them through!

They're the palette....

that
makes you
YOU.